Mommy, Can I EAT this?

Ms. Maria S

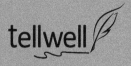

Tellwell Talent
www.tellwell.ca

ISBN
978-0-2288-0166-5 (Hardcover)
978-0-2288-0165-8 (Paperback)

This book is dedicated to you, Papa. Your journey and battle reignited my passion for nutrition and inspired me to help others. In losing you, I realized I wanted to mentor and help people. As the Buddhist saying goes, "When the student is ready the teacher will appear."

This book is also dedicated to my family, loved ones, and soul sisters.

Lastly, this book is dedicated to you, Mama. You have always inspired me with your examples of good nutrition. Your strength completely amazes me. Even in complete darkness and devastation, you remain strong.

"Do you know what day it is today? It's Momtastic Monday," said Mommy. "Do you know what game we are going to play today? The sugar cube game."

"Sugar cube game?" asked Ariel and Michael. "What is that?"

Mommy said, "Every day, I will give you each 5 sugar cubes. Open your hands and let's count together: 1, 2, 3, 4, 5 ... When you eat a sugary treat, Mommy will take away your sugar cubes. The more sugar cubes you have left at the end of the week, the bigger the super-duper, fancy treat you will get. Are you ready to play the sugar cube game?"

"We are ready," said Ariel and Michael.

Parents' and Teachers' Corner 🍎

As of July 2018, the Food and Drug Administration requires manufacturers to show on food labels not just all sugars, but also those that were added (*Heart Insight Magazine*, 2017, para. 9).

Did you know? 💡 Updated in 2018, The American Heart Association recommends that children should consume less than 25 grams of added sugars per day, which is equal to 6 teaspoons (para.1).

Rules of the Sugar Cube Game!

Limit is 5 sugar cubes a day per child. Each sugar cube is 4 grams of sugar and in total equals 20 grams. Each treat in this book has been rounded down. Children are only allowed to eat the amount they have earned in sugar cubes.

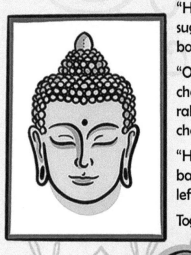

"Happy Tasty Tuesday," said Mommy. "Today, you get another 5 sugar cubes. Let's count together: 1, 2, 3, 4, 5. So now, you should both have 10 sugar cubes."

"Oh my goodness," said Ariel, "I can see with my big brown eyes, chocolate chip cookies! Mmm, I want cookies. Cookies, Cookies, rah, rah, rah, cookies, cookies, ha, ha, ha! Mommy, can I eat the chocolate chip cookie?" asked Ariel.

"Hmm," said Mommy. "If you eat this cookie, you will have to give back 3 sugar cubes. That means you will only have 7 sugar cubes left for today."

Together, they said, "No. We want to save for our super-duper, fancy treat."

= 10

"Happy Wonderful Wednesday! You get another 5 sugar cubes. Let's count together: 1, 2, 3, 4, 5. So now, you should both have 15 sugar cubes."

"Ohh," said Michael. "I have a yum, yum in my tum, tum, for that chocolate bar sitting on the counter. Oh Mommy, can I eat this chocolate bar?" asked Michael.

"Hmm, if you eat this chocolate bar," said Mommy, "you will have to give me 8 sugar cubes, which means you will only have 7 sugar cubes left for today. It's your choice. What would you like to do?"

"But why do we have to lose so many sugar cubes?" asked Michael. "We will have nothing left. It's not fair. We love chocolate, and it tastes so good."

"Remember the rules," said Mommy. "Too much chocolate will make your tummy hurt."

Ariel and Michael began crying. "But Mommy, it's not fair, we want chocolate."

Michael wondered how he could eat the chocolate bar and still keep his cubes.

Michael said to himself, *there must be a way to save my cubes and eat my treats.*

Parents' and Teachers' Corner 🍎

Kids between 2-18 should have less than 25 grams of sugar daily or 6 teaspoons daily according to the scientific statement recommending a specific limit on added sugars for children, published in the American Heart Association journal *Circulation*.

"The National Cancer Institute also found that 14- to 18-year-old children consume the most added sugar on a daily basis, averaging about 34.3 teaspoons" (Hutton, 2016, para. 9).

Did you know? 💡 According to an article published in *Heart Insight Magazine*, Johnson, a professor of nutrition and pediatrics at the University of Vermont in Burlington, affirmed that "Children are developing eating habits and taste preferences that will last a lifetime. The sooner families begin to limit the amount of added sugars in their diets, the better" (2017, para. 6).

Michael really wanted the chocolate bar and decided to hide in the corner and eat a little tiny piece and another tiny piece until it was all gone. Mommy surely wouldn't notice a missing chocolate bar.

But Mommy did notice because Michael had chocolate all over his face, and she found Michael crying because his tummy was hurting.

"Oh Michael," said Mommy, "when you eat too much sugar, your tummy will hurt."

"I am sorry, Mommy. I promise I won't do it again. I really want my super-duper fancy treat and I am trying my best."

"Well, since you cheated," said Mommy, "you will lose three sugar cubes, but if you stay on track, you could still win the super-duper, fancy treat this week. I know this is not easy, but Mommy knows you are trying your best!"

Parents' and Teachers' Corner 🍎

Healthy Tip: Small doses of sugar do provide your child with energy. It's important to provide nutritious sources of sugar. The sugars found in fruits, vegetables, and dairy foods are natural, which means they should have a prominent spot in your child's healthy eating plan.

Did you know? 💡 What is dangerous to your child's health is added sugar, which is found in desserts, soda, and baked goods, according to MayoClinic.com (Ipaptenco, 2018, para. 3).

"Happy Thankful Thursday," said Mommy. "You get another 5 sugar cubes. Let's count together: 1, 2, 3, 4, 5. Ariel has 20 sugar cubes and Michael has 17."

"Ohh look, I can see with my big brown eyes vanilla ice cream in the freezer," said Ariel. "Mommy, can I have some vanilla ice cream?"

"Hmm," said Mommy. "That means you would lose all five of your sugar cubes for today."

Ariel looked sad, but decided she didn't want to use her sugar cubes.

"Happy Fun Friday," said Mommy, "and you get another 5 sugar cubes. Let's count: 1, 2, 3, 4, 5 together. Ariel has 25 sugar cubes and Michael has 22."

"Yum, yum, yum in my tum, tum, tum," said Michael. "Fizzy pop. I love bubbles! Mommy, can I drink a can of pop? I really want it, Mommy."

Mommy answered, "You will lose 9 sugar cubes. Are you really sure you want to lose that many of your sugar cubes for a can of fizzy pop?"

The children looked at each other and said, "No way, we are going to play. We are so close to winning that super-duper fancy treat."

Michael asked Ariel, "What do you think the super-duper treat will be? A trip to the zoo, a trip to the aquarium?"

"Happy Sunshine Saturday!" said Mommy. "And you get another 5 sugar cubes. Let's count together: 1, 2, 3, 4, 5. Ariel, you have 30 sugar cubes, and Michael, you have 27."

"Mommy, can I eat this box of chocolate candy?" asked Ariel.

"Hmm," said Mommy. "If you eat that box of chocolate candy, you will have to give me 8 sugar cubes."

"Oh boy," said Ariel and Michael. "We are so close to the super-duper treat, we will wait, Mommy."

"Let me show you what could happen to your teeth if you eat too much candy. You will have to visit the dentist and get your tooth pulled out because you will get a cavity."

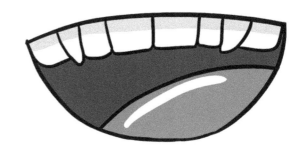

Parents' and Teachers' Corner 🍎

On average, a box of chocolate candy has 35 grams of sugar and weighs 73 grams. In this example, the children would lose 8 sugar cubes. Health Tip: Try to offer children naturally sweet and healthy snacks like fruit. You could also make a smoothie or popsicle out of natural juice.

Did you know? 💡 "The mouth is full of hundreds of bacteria, many of which are beneficial to the oral ecosystem. However, certain harmful oral bacteria actually feed on the sugars you eat to create acids that destroy the tooth enamel, which is the shiny, protective outer layer of the tooth" (Stapleton, 2019, para.2).

"But Mommy, do you think we will ever eat a chocolate chip cookie again?"

"Hmm," Mommy said. "Well, I know how much you both love chocolate, so let's bake chocolate chip cookies together. If we bake them ourselves and put a little less sugar in, you will have a healthier treat."

The children were so excited to bake with their mommy.

Parents' and Teachers' Corner 🍎

Health Tip: Baking with your children allows you to control the sugar content and teach your children how to take control of their sugar content.

Did you know? 💡 "Other tips for cutting back on foods with added sugars include avoiding sweet processed foods, which tend to be loaded with added sugars, such as cereal bars, cookies, cakes and many foods marketed specifically to children, like sweet cereals (American Heart Association, 2016, para. 19)."

"There are over 56 names of sugar hidden in foods that your children are eating" (Richards, 2017, para. 5).

"Yahoo, you made it! It's Sunday," said Mommy, "and you get 5 sugar cubes each. Let's count: 1,2,3,4,5. Ariel, you have 35, and Michael, you have 32 sugar cubes. Yahoo! Mommy is so proud of you both!"

"Let's play next week and the week after!" screamed Ariel and Michael. "Sugar cubes, sugar cubes, sugar cubes, yah!"

"But Mommy, what is the super-duper fancy treat you promised us? Is it a trip to the zoo? Is it a trip to the aquarium or to the movies?"

"Hmm," Mommy said. "Since you did so well, you can pick where you would like to go."

Ariel and Michael screamed, "Yahoo! We want to go to the zoo!"

Ariel and Michael asked Mommy, "Next year when we are older, can you teach us how to read labels and visit the grocery store?"

"Yes," said Mommy. "I would love to take you on an adventure ride through the grocery store." Stay tuned!

Parents' and Teachers' Corner 🍎

Recommended Food Servings for Children

Dairy: 2 or less servings daily; Grains: 5 or less servings daily; Lean meats and poultry, fish, eggs, tofu, nuts and seeds: 2-3 serving daily; Fruits, vegetables, legumes and beans: intake of vegetables should be 3-5 servings (Children's Health, n.d., para. 4).

Did you know? 💡 Remember: everything in moderation. Children should enjoy a balanced diet, which includes sugar, but make sure you know their daily allowance! I hope my book has inspired you to take action in learning more about your children's intake allowances.

Contest for Parents

Thank you for purchasing a copy of my book. Please register by visiting my website at www.amorelivelife.com. Once registered you will also receive more details on quarterly contests.

Contest for Teachers

Thank you for purchasing a copy of my book. Please register by visiting my website at www.amorelivelife.com. Once registered you will also receive more details on quarterly contests towards classroom activities and books.

About the Author

Maria is passionate about holistic nutrition and energy healing. As someone who has struggled with weight and has had to overcome an addiction to sugar, she has made it her life's mission to educate parents and teachers on the importance of teaching nutrition to young children.

Maria's mother operated a subsidized daycare for over 30 years. She cooked every meal from scratch for the kids because she believed in the importance of healthy nutrition. She instilled in Maria that parents have an obligation to give children the best foods at an early age to optimize and boost their immune system.

Through loss after loss, especially her father's death, Maria realized how vital a role nutrition plays, including in illness.

Maria received her certification as an angel intuitive. From there, she obtained diplomas in angel and animal reiki, as well as intuitive healing, medical intuition, and meditation. Maria also holds a diploma in holistic nutrition as a health coach. Maria is also continuing her education, specializing in holistic health to obtain her PhD. Her mandate is to educate children about nutrition, so they have a blueprint with which to make better choices throughout their lives.

REFERENCES

American Heart Association. (2017). "Kids and sugar." Retrieved from
    heartinsight.heart.org/Spring-2017/Kids-and-Sugar/

"Children should eat less than 25 grams of added sugars daily." (2016). Retrieved from
    newsroom.heart.org/news/children-should-eat-less-than-25-grams-of-added-sugars-daily

Cleveland Clinic. (2018). "Sugar: How bad are sweets for your kids?" Retrieved from
    health.clevelandclinic.org/sugar-how-bad-are-sweets-for-your-kids/

Children's Health. (n.d.). "Recommended serving size." Retrieved from www.childrens.
    com/ health-wellness/recommended-serving-size-by-age

Cohen, D. (2019). "Why kids need to spend time in nature." Retrieved from childmind.
    org/article/why-kids-need-to-spend-time-in-nature/

Hutton, L. (2019). "Are we too sweet? Our kids' addiction to sugar." Retrieved from
    www.familyeducation.com/life/sugar/are-we-too-sweet-our-kids-addiction-sugar

Ipatenco, S. (2018). "What is the maximum amount of sugar a day for children?" Retrieved from
    healthyeating.sfgate.com/maximum-amount-sugar-day-children-8982.html

Johnson, R. et al. (2019). "Dietary sugars intake and cardiovascular health." Retrieved from
    circ.ahajournals.org/content/circulation/120/11/1011.full.pdf

MacMillan, A. (2018). "Here's the Max Amount of Sugar Kids Should Really Have In a Day."
    Retrieved from www.health.com/nutrition/kids-sugar-recommendations

McGinn, D. (2017). "Canadian children are consuming five times more sugar than they should." Retrieved from www.theglobeandmail.com/life/health-and-fitness/ health/ canadian-children-are-consuming-five-times-more-sugar-than-they-should/ article35207835/

Richards, L. (2017). "56 names for sugar: Are you eating more than you realize?" Retrieved from https://www.thecandidadiet.com/56-names-sugar-eating-realize/

Stapleton, K. (2019). "What are the effects of sugar on teeth?" Retrieved from www.colgate. com/ en-us/oral-health/conditions/cavities/what-are-the-effects-of-sugar-on-teeth-1214

CPSIA information can be obtained
at www.ICGtesting.com
Printed in the USA
LVHW012244300519
619685LV00034B/1010/P